The Three Roses

Olivier Bonnewijn – Amandine Wanert

THE ADVENTURES OF JAMIE AND BELLA

The Three Roses

MAGNIFICAT. - Ignatius

Table of Contents

Chapter 1 "Please, Bella!"

The Biltons lived in a cozy little house on Hempton Street. Jamie and Bella each had a bedroom under the roof; the twins were ten-and-a-half years old, and each was happy to have a small space to call his own. Lily and Bubba, their younger siblings, shared a large bedroom on the floor below. Their small beds seemed to float like lifeboats upon a sea of toys.

After school one day, Bella sat at her desk, doing her homework. She was struggling with a difficult math problem: How many minutes does it take to fill a bathtub with forty-two gallons of water if seven gallons come out of the faucet every minute?

"Wouldn't it be easier just to ask a plumber or to take a bath to find out?" sighed Bella, trying to focus. Caught up in her thoughts, she did not notice that Lily had opened the door a crack and was peering in with a sheepish smile.

"Hey, Bellaaaaaaa," she said.

"You scared me," answered Bella, jumping up. "I've asked you a hundred times to knock before coming in," she continued, slightly annoyed.

"Oops, sorry, I forgot. Can you play with me?" asked Lily.

"Not now," Bella replied. "I've got to finish this problem set for tomorrow."

"Please," insisted Lily.

"No, maybe later," Bella answered.

"Oh, please, Bella, please can you play now?" persisted Lily.

"Okay, fine," said Bella, closing her notebook and getting up.

"You're the best!" said Lily, beaming.

Lily dragged a large bag into the middle of the room and dumped a dozen stuffed animals onto

the carpet. She placed her bear Honeyball on the bed next to Iceberg the penguin. She then seated her three dolls and two baby seals comfortably in a row in front of the others.

Next she took a ruler and said with a serious face, "School is starting! Class, be quiet! Bella, sit down in your chair."

Bella rolled her eyes. She hated being bossed around by her seven-year-old sister. She also

wanted to read the magazine that her friend Zoe had lent her. It had an article about wild horses in Wyoming and the people trying to protect them. Despite her wandering thoughts, she kindly sat in the chair Lily pointed out to her. Bella had a big heart.

Soon both girls were having so much fun playing that they completely lost track of time.

"It's already six!" exclaimed Bella all of a sudden, looking at her watch. "Lily, would you mind leaving me now?"

"Why?" asked Lily.

"Because," said Bella.

"Because what?" continued Lily.

"Because I need time alone," responded Bella.

"But class is not finished. Please let me stay a little longer," Lily pleaded.

"No, it's recess time! Everyone outside."

Bella gently led Lily out and closed her door.

Stepping over a couple of stuffed animals, she made her way to the corner of her room. There lay the wooden box her dad had once used to store tools in the garage.

Chapter 2 # Silence of the Heart

O n the box was a delicate lace cloth. Bella had placed on it the statue of our Lady that she had received for her First Communion from her godmother. Bella had also put a crucifix and a rosary on the box, along with a candle that she was not allowed to light. A very old Bible lay to the left of the statue; it had once belonged to her grandparents.

There were also two framed pictures on the box: one of Bella and her friends at the playground and the other of her entire family at the beach. Inside the box were a secret notebook in which Bella wrote her inmost thoughts, a songbook and a pile of notecards and letters she had received from friends and relatives. Bella tended this prayer corner with love and care.

As she did nearly every evening, Bella knelt in front of her little altar. She turned toward God in body, heart and spirit. She slowly made the Sign of the Cross:

"In the name of the Father, and of the Son, and of the Holy Spirit. Amen."

Putting her hands together and looking at the statue of Mary, she softly prayed:

"Hail Mary, full of grace, the Lord is with thee. Blessed art thou among women, and blessed is the fruit of thy womb, Jesus."

Bella also recited a prayer she had learned in her catechism class:

"Lord Jesus, you who are infinite love, give me the grace to love like you. Fill my heart with joy to sing your praises. Make my hands ready to serve. Let my eyes see you in others. Open my ears so I can hear your voice. Let me always live in your light."

Bella opened her heart to God's presence within her as she prayed. She then spoke to the Lord as she would to a friend:

"Thank you, Lord Jesus, for being here with me. Thank you for Zoe. She kindly lent me her magazine today. I pray for Grammy, whose hip was operated on last week. All went well, thank you.

And how about you, Lord? You must have been saddened by the explosion I heard about on the radio. I pray for those who caused the explosion but especially for those who were injured and those who died."

Bella was seated now, and she no longer spoke. She was flooded with peace and entirely focused on Jesus. She closed her eyes, and the peaceful silence of God filled her whole being. She wanted to welcome the Lord into her soul. He came, and Bella greeted him with pure faith.

Chapter 3 Distractions

All of a sudden, Iceberg the penguin flashed into Bella's mind. "Poor thing," she thought. "His wing is torn and needs to be sewn up again. The stuffing is coming out. Lily should not have swung him at Jamie when she was angry the other day. She needs to control her temper. The next time she—" Bella abruptly stopped her thoughts.

"Oh, sorry, Lord. I was distracted," she said in prayer and was quickly led back into the silence of her heart with Jesus.

Several seconds later, however, her thoughts went elsewhere again. She saw in her mind a large chocolate cake waiting to be devoured. "What fun it was to bake that cake with Mom," she told herself. "Thank goodness I was there, otherwise Mom

would have put in those awful nuts that I hate. I hope we will also have vanilla ice cream tonight. We had chocolate cake and ice cream at Zoe's birthday party. Yum!"

Soon Bella realized that she was letting her thoughts carry her away.

"I'm sorry, Lord. Again I got distracted," she admitted.

Without feeling discouraged, she once more turned her heart to God. She didn't feel his presence as strongly as before, but she felt a great peace. She continued her prayer, and with eyes fixed on the crucifix, she whispered:

"My Lord, I believe in you. My God, I love you."

Bella's mind again went astray a minute later. She remembered last weekend at her cousin's house. "Mandy's rabbit is so cute," she thought. It escaped, and she and Mandy happily ran after it.

Then the neighbors' big dog jumped out and started chasing them. "We were so frightened, we were screaming our heads off," thought Bella. "Good thing Uncle Bill came to our rescue—"

"Oh, Lord, I'm sorry. I was distracted once again!" Bella exclaimed.

Without a moment's hesitation, she returned her thoughts to Jesus alone. As she concentrated on him, she became very much aware of his presence. But then Jesus seemed not as close as he was before. She felt as if God was playing hide-and-seek with her.

Chapter 4 The Dawn Visitor

Bella finished her prayer in the same way she had started it, by making the Sign of the Cross:

"In the name of the Father, and of the Son and of the Holy Spirit. Amen."

At that moment, someone knocked at her door. "Come in," called Bella, quickly getting up and moving toward the door.

"Hi, it's me!" cried Lily happily. "Dinner is ready."

"Great. I'll come down right away," replied Bella.

"Bella?" said Lily sweetly.

"What is it, Lily?" Bella asked.

"Thanks for playing with me earlier. I love you!" Lily cried out.

After dinner that evening, the children went upstairs to their bedrooms. By the time Dad and Mom came to kiss the children goodnight, Bella had finished her math problems. She lay on her bed, reading Zoe's magazine with delight. She soon felt tired, turned off her light and fell asleep.

At the crack of dawn, when the Biltons were still sleeping, Bella had a beautiful dream. She saw hundreds of rays of intense light beam through the door of her room.

A mysterious figure came toward her from this cloud of light. He held three beautiful roses.

"Hello, Bella!" said the unexpected visitor.

"Hi," said Bella hesitantly.

"Don't you recognize me?" asked the stranger, smiling gently.

"Uh, yes, sort of . . . Umm, no . . . Uh, not really," faltered Bella.

"I'm Jesus," the young boy said.

"Jesus!" exclaimed Bella.

"I want to thank you for these lovely roses. They really made me happy," Jesus said.

"Thank me? For the roses?" answered a confused Bella.

"Yes," said Jesus. "You gave me these roses. During your prayer this evening, you were distracted three times. Remember?" Jesus asked.

Bella, still dreaming, was dumbfounded. She did not understand.

"You really like it when I'm distracted during prayer, Lord?" inquired Bella, increasingly surprised.

"Oh, that doesn't matter," said Jesus.

"Really?" replied Bella.

"Yes. Three times during your prayer you said, 'Sorry, Lord. I was distracted.' Three times you stopped the thoughts spinning around in your mind to be with me. Three times you came running back to me. I was so happy to receive these three beautiful flowers with their sweet perfume as a gift," Jesus said.

"Wow. I didn't know that," Bella answered. "Next time, perhaps I can give you a whole bouquet," she said joyfully.

Christ smiled as she spoke, and Bella knew that he loved her. She realized that Jesus knew and understood her better than anyone else did,

even better than her own parents did. While he looked at her happily, he slowly disappeared into a heavenly light. Bella's heart overflowed with such an intense joy that she woke up.

She opened the curtains and sat on a chair near her window. Outside, the birds were chirping loudly. Bella watched the sun slowly rise and remained in the peaceful presence of her very special guest.

Reading Key: To Better Understand the Story

1. **Why does Bella push Lily out of her room in the story?**

Jesus says: "When you pray, go into your room and shut the door and pray to your Father who is in secret; and your Father who sees in secret will reward you" (Matthew 6:6). Bella is simply following the Lord's advice given in the Gospel. She stops playing, even though she is enjoying herself, and asks her little sister to leave the room. She wants to converse with the Lord "in secret."

2. Bella made a prayer corner in her bedroom. Why?

It is possible to pray anywhere: in the street, on the playground, in the woods, at the dinner table or at your desk. Nonetheless, Bella wanted to have in her room a special spot for God alone. Her prayer corner serves as a constant reminder of the Lord's presence and helps Bella to pray more frequently and to stay longer in his company.

3. Isn't it enough just to go to Mass and pray with my family?

Yes, this is probably sufficient when you are little. When Bella was five, she prayed nearly every evening with her family or in her bed with her mom or dad. But now that she's older, she enjoys spending time alone with the Lord. Sometimes it is easy and sometimes it is harder, but she is always glad to make God happy. Since she began this time of personal prayer, she has enjoyed going to Mass much more.

4. **How does Bella pray?**

• First, she turns to God in silence and then makes the Sign of the Cross.

• While looking intently at the statue of our Lady or the crucifix, she recites special prayers with much love, concentrating on the words.

• She then speaks to the Lord as to a friend, using her own words. She tells him about her day, thanks him, asks him for things, confides her worries and her joys to him and tells him she's sorry for any wrong she may have done that day.

• A period of silence follows. She dwells close to God under his loving gaze, remaining in his presence.

• She finishes her prayer by joyfully making the Sign of the Cross.

5. **Could Bella have prayed differently?**

Yes, of course.

• Sometimes, she takes her songbook out of the box and sings (never loudly enough for Jamie to hear her, though).

• She also often reads passages from the Bible or a book about a saint.

• Occasionally she writes a prayer, a poem or a thought in her secret notebook.

• She always leaves a few minutes to listen to our Lord in silence. This is her favorite moment. She says nothing. She is there, God is there, and that is all that matters.

And what about you? How do you pray?

6. Where can I find the "silence of the heart" spoken of in the story?

The heart of every child and adult is like a big house. Some rooms are quiet; others are noisy. When Bella prays, she enters this interior house and goes straight to the quietest room by the garden, without paying attention to the noisy rooms on the side. She remains in this peaceful place and waits attentively for her Lord to come and visit: "Behold, I stand at the door and knock; if any one hears my voice and opens the door, I will come in" (Revelation 3:20).

7. Why does Bella get distracted?

It is completely normal to get distracted during prayer. As Bella's will and spirit are focused entirely on God, her imagination is let free and sometimes leads her thoughts elsewhere.

8. What should I do when I get distracted during prayer?

• Return to God as quickly as possible. You can say, for example, "My Lord, I believe in you. My God, I love you."

• The source of your distraction can also be turned into a prayer. Bella could have said, "Lord, I pray for Uncle Bill, who caught Mandy's rabbit and scared off that big dog. Please help him find a good job."

• Try not to get discouraged. You can also use your watch and tell the Lord you will give him six minutes of your time, for instance. This can help fight off distractions.

9. Is it really important to stay for some time in God's presence?

Yes, it is. God wants to have time to visit and transform us with his love. Bella understands this. She spends several minutes in his company. These minutes are filled with faith, hope and love. In this way, God gives us his life and his light to us.

10. There are times when it is more difficult to "see God." Why is this?

"Our eyes are like those of an owl gazing at the sun," writes Saint John of the Cross. God is infinitely more brilliant than the sun. Our eyes, like those of the night owl, are not accustomed to such brightness. During our time on earth, our sight must be adjusted, purified and transformed by the light of our faith in Jesus, who is true God and true man. This is why Bella sometimes feels as if she does not perceive much in prayer. But it does not prevent her from communicating with God. Quite the contrary!

11. What is most important in prayer?

God is! We pray to please our Lord. Jesus smiles radiantly at Bella in her dream. This is proof that her prayer made him very happy. Do you have a special way of making our Lord smile? You can soon discover if you do by trying!

12. Is a dream like Bella's really possible?

Yes, it is. Jesus can visit you in your sleep. This kind of dream is rare, however.

The Author

Olivier Bonnewijn

Father Olivier Bonnewijn has been a priest of the Archdiocese of Brussels in Belgium since 1993 and is a member of the Emmanuel Community. He teaches at the Institute for Theological Studies in Brussels.

The Adventures of Jamie and Bella were conceived during summer catechetical camps. The children's thirst for truth and their contagious enthusiasm inspired the stories, which are all based on true accounts. Father Bonnewijn had the joy of witnessing many of them.

The Illustrator

Amandine Wanert

Amandine Wanert lives in Paris. She illustrates both for medical journals and for children's literature. Fascinated by the world of children, she spends time observing them in public parks and in school settings to fuel her imagination. Jamie's and Bella's physical features are in part based on her childhood memories. Bringing to life The Adventures of Jamie and Bella in harmony with Father Bonnewijn's text has been a joyful and enriching experience for Amandine.

Translated by Marthe-Marie Lebbe
Cover illustration by Amandine Wanert

Original French edition:
Les aventures de Jojo et Gaufrette : Les trois roses
© 2009 by Édition de l'Emmanuel, Paris
© 2013 by MAGNIFICAT, New York • Ignatius Press, San Francisco
All rights reserved.
ISBN Ignatius Press 978-1-58617-812-3 • ISBN MAGNIFICAT 978-1-936260-56-0
The trademark MAGNIFICAT depicted in this publication is used under license
from and is the exclusive property of MAGNIFICAT Central Service Team, Inc.,
A Ministry to Catholic Women, and may not be used without its written consent.

Printed by Pollina on December 4, 2012
Job Number MGN 12016
Printed in France, in compliance with the Consumer Protection Safety Act of 2008.